CAPYBARAS

by Allan Morey

AMICUS HIGH INTEREST • AMICUS INK

Amicus High Interest and Amicus Ink are imprints of Amicus
P.O. Box 1329, Mankato, MN 56002
www.amicuspublishing.us

Library of Congress Cataloging-in-Publication Data
Names: Morey, Allan, author.
Title: Capybaras / by Allan Morey.
Description: Mankato, Minnesota : Amicus High Interest, [2018] |
 Series: Weird and unusual animals | Audience: K to grade 3. | Includes
 bibliographical references and index.
Identifiers: LCCN 2016038829 (print) | LCCN 2016052987 (ebook) |
 ISBN 9781681511559 (library binding) | ISBN 9781681521862 (pbk.) |
 ISBN 9781681512457 (ebook)
Subjects: LCSH: Capybara--Juvenile literature. | Rodents--Juvenile
literature.
Classification: LCC QL737.R662 M67 2018 (print) | LCC QL737.R662
(ebook) | DDC 599.35/9--dc23
LC record available at https://lccn.loc.gov/2016038829

Photo Credits: tets/Shutterstock background pattern; Sean Crane/
Minden Pictures cover photo; Volga2012/iStock 2; Maxym Boner/iStock
4-5; Stephen Iles/Alamy Stock Photo 7; Berndt Fischer/Age Fotostock
8-9; Jami Tarris/Corbis Documentary/Getty 11; Gerard Lacz/Gerard Lacz
Images/Superstock 12-13; Bruno Vieira/Shutterstock 14-15; Juergen
Ritterbach/vario images GmbH & Co.KG/Alamy Stock Photo 16-17;
Oakdalecat/Dreamstime.com 19; stephenmeese/iStock 20-21; anankkml/
iStock 22

Editor: Wendy Dieker
Designer: Aubrey Harper
Photo Researcher: Holly Young

Printed in the
United States of America

HC 10 9 8 7 6 5 4 3 2 1
PB 10 9 8 7 6 5 4 3 2 1

TABLE OF CONTENTS

4

WORLD'S BIGGEST RODENTS

Tiny mice are **rodents**. Rabbits and squirrels are, too. And so are huge capybaras! These rodents live in Central and South America. They can be as big as large dogs.

WETLAND HOMES

Capybaras live in wet places.
They spend a lot of time in the
water. They wade in lakes. They
swim in rivers. They roll in mud
to stay cool.

GREAT SWIMMERS

Capybaras are great swimmers. They have **webbed feet**. Their eyes and noses are on the tops of their heads. This helps them see and breathe as they swim.

Weird but True
Capybaras can hold their breath for up to five minutes.

BIG TEETH

Capybaras have sharp front teeth.

These teeth are used for **gnawing**.

They can cut through tough plants.

Capybaras eat water plants.

STAYING SAFE

Capybaras jump into the water when there is danger. They swim away from wild cats. They duck under the water to hide from eagles. **Caiman** and snakes also hunt them.

Weird but True
Some people hunt capybaras for their meat.

PUPS

A female capybara gives birth to two to eight babies at a time. Babies are called pups. Pups look like small **adults**. They stay with their mothers. They learn what plants to eat.

FAMILY GROUPS

Capybaras live in family groups.

Groups have about 20 members.

A large male is the leader. All of

the females care for the pups.

NOISY ANIMALS

Capybaras make a lot of noises.

It is how they talk to each other.

They bark when danger is near.

They also whistle, chirp, and growl.

Pups purr to their mothers.

WATER PIGS

Capybaras have a funny **nickname**. People used to think they were pigs. So they were called water pigs. They are big and round like a pig, but they swim. The funny name fits!

A LOOK AT CAPYBARAS

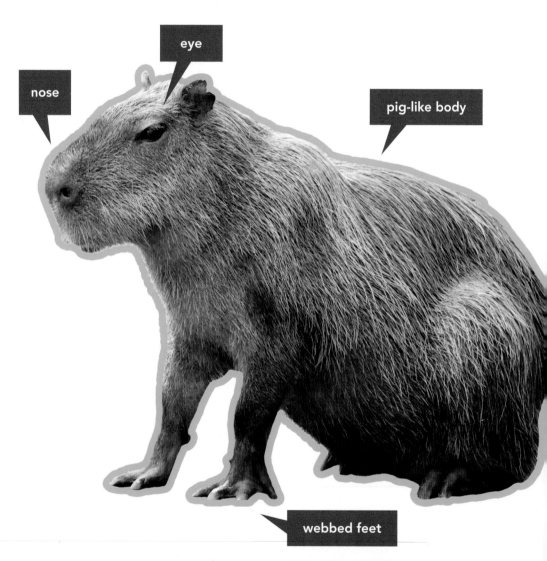

WORDS TO KNOW

adult – an animal that is fully grown

caiman – a small alligator-like reptile

gnawing – chewing and biting

nickname – another name for a person or animal

rodent – small mammals with sharp front teeth used for gnawing; mice, rats, beavers, and capybaras are all rodents.

webbed feet – to have feet with a thin layer of skin connecting the toes

LEARN MORE

Books
Borgert-Spaniol, Megan. *Capybaras*. Minneapolis: Bellwether Media Inc., 2014.

Niver, Heather Moore. *Capybaras after Dark*. New York: Enslow Publishing, 2017.

Websites
Rain Forest Alliance—Capybara
www.rainforest-alliance.org/kids/species-profiles/capybara

San Diego Zoo—Capybara
http://animals.sandiegozoo.org/animals/capybara

INDEX